Dear Parent:
Your child's love of reading starts here!

Every child learns to read in a different way and at his or her own speed. Some go back and forth between reading levels and read favorite books again and again. Others read through each level in order. You can help your young reader improve and become more confident by encouraging his or her own interests and abilities. From books your child reads with you to the first books he or she reads alone, there are I Can Read Books for every stage of reading:

SHARED READING
Basic language, word repetition, and whimsical illustrations, ideal for sharing with your emergent reader

BEGINNING READING
Short sentences, familiar words, and simple concepts for children eager to read on their own

READING WITH HELP
Engaging stories, longer sentences, and language play for developing readers

READING ALONE
Complex plots, challenging vocabulary, and high-interest topics for the independent reader

ADVANCED READING
Short paragraphs, chapters, and exciting themes for the perfect bridge to chapter books

I Can Read Books have introduced children to the joy of reading since 1957. Featuring award-winning authors and illustrators and a fabulous cast of beloved characters, I Can Read Books set the standard for beginning readers.

A lifetime of discovery begins with the magical words "I Can Read!"

Visit www.icanread.com for information
on enriching your child's reading experience.

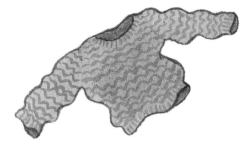

For Peter and Laura
—A.S.C.

Biscuit and the Lost Teddy Bear   Text copyright © 2011 by Alyssa Satin Capucilli   Illustrations copyright © 2011 by Pat Schories
All rights reserved. Manufactured in China. No part of this book may be used or reproduced in any manner whatsoever
without written permission except in the case of brief quotations embodied in critical articles and reviews. For information
address HarperCollins Children's Books, a division of HarperCollins Publishers, 10 East 53rd Street, New York, NY 10022.
www.icanread.com

Library of Congress Cataloging-in-Publication Data is available.
ISBN 978-0-06-117751-4 (trade bdg.) — ISBN 978-0-06-117753-8 (pbk.)

12 13 14 15   SCP   10 9 8 7 6 5 4   ❖   First Edition

Biscuit and the Lost Teddy Bear

story by ALYSSA SATIN CAPUCILLI
pictures by PAT SCHORIES

HARPER
An Imprint of HarperCollinsPublishers

Woof, woof!

What do you see, Biscuit?

Is it a bird?

Woof, woof!

Is it a butterfly?
Woof, woof!

Oh, Biscuit.

It is a teddy bear!

Woof, woof!

Someone lost a teddy bear.

Who can it be?

Woof, woof!

Woof, woof!

Is this your teddy bear, Sam?

Ruff!

No. It is not Sam's bear.

Woof, woof!

Is this your teddy bear, Puddles?

Bow wow!

No. It is not Puddles's bear.

Woof, woof!

Someone lost a teddy bear.

But who can it be?

Woof, woof!

Wait, Biscuit.

What do you see now?

Woof!

Biscuit sees a big truck.

Woof!

Biscuit sees a lot of boxes.

Woof, woof!

Biscuit sees a little boy, too.

Woof, woof! Woof, woof!
Is this your teddy bear,
little boy?

Yes. It is!

Woof!

The little boy
lost his teddy bear, Biscuit,
but you found it!
Woof, woof!

The teddy bear gets a big hug.

Woof, woof!

And Biscuit gets a big hug, too!
Woof!

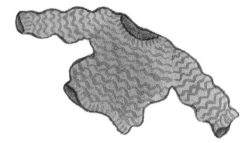

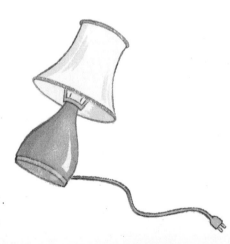